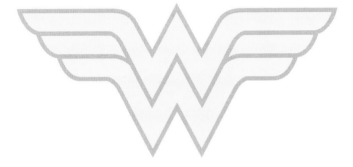

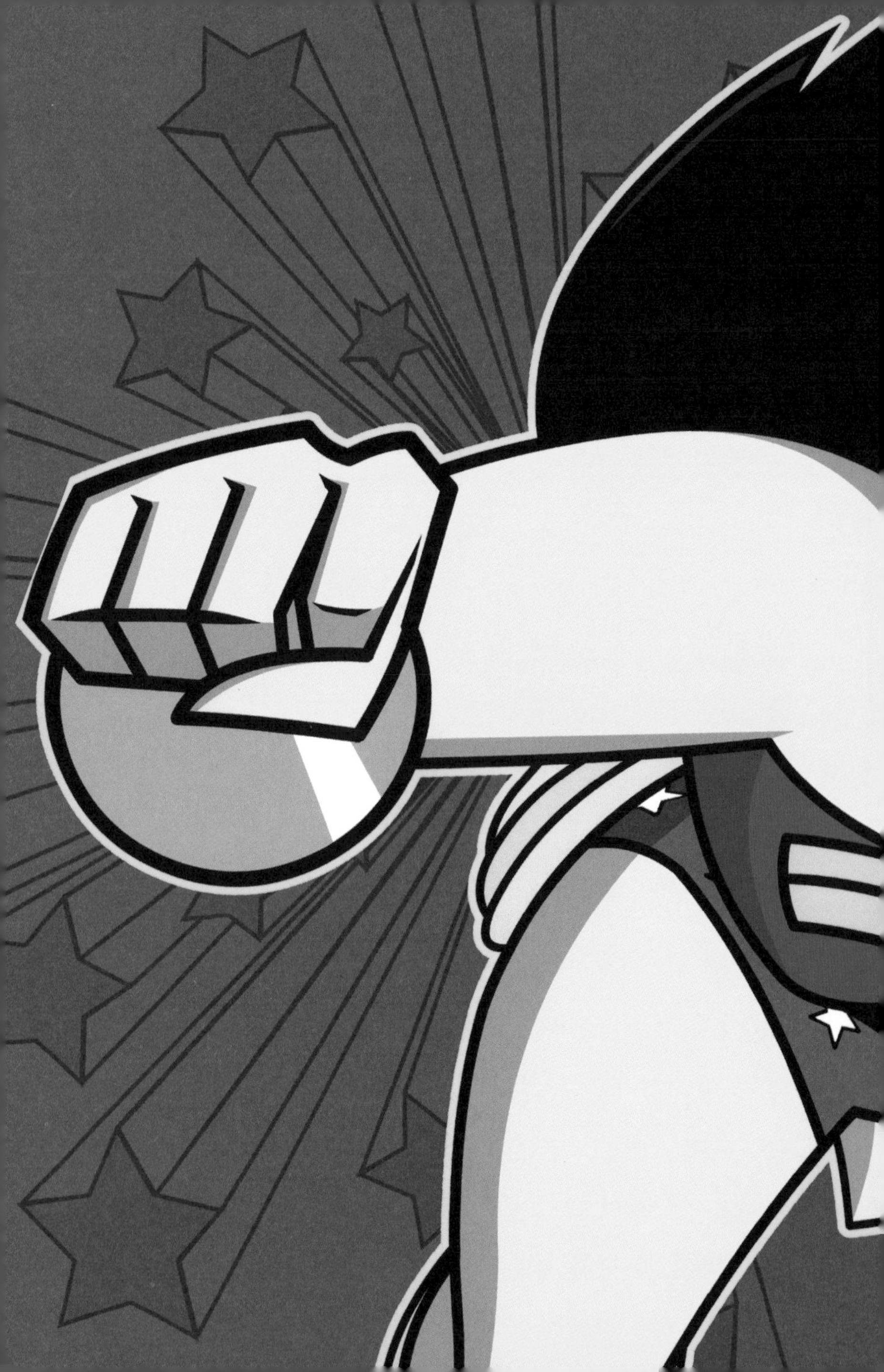

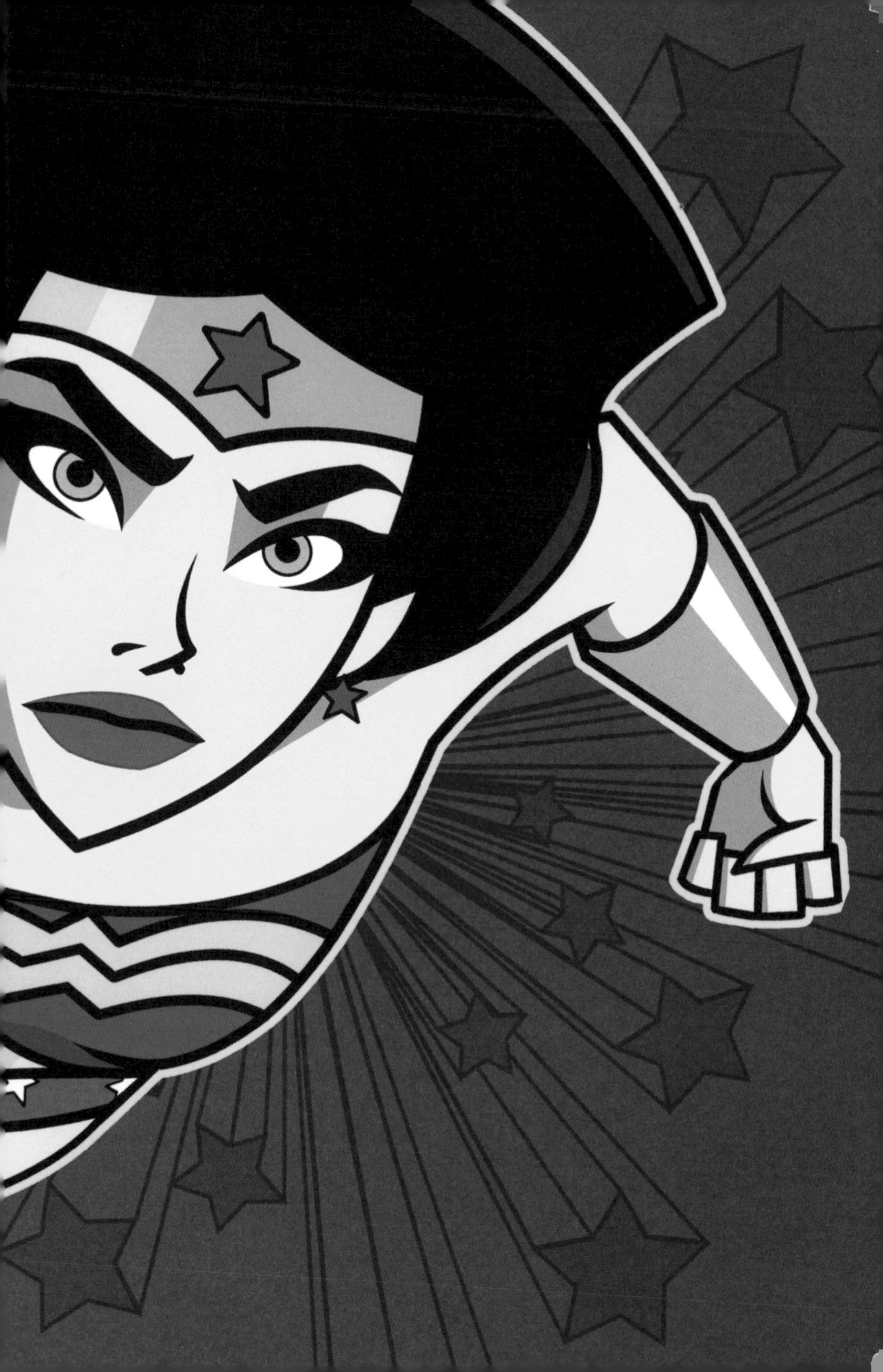

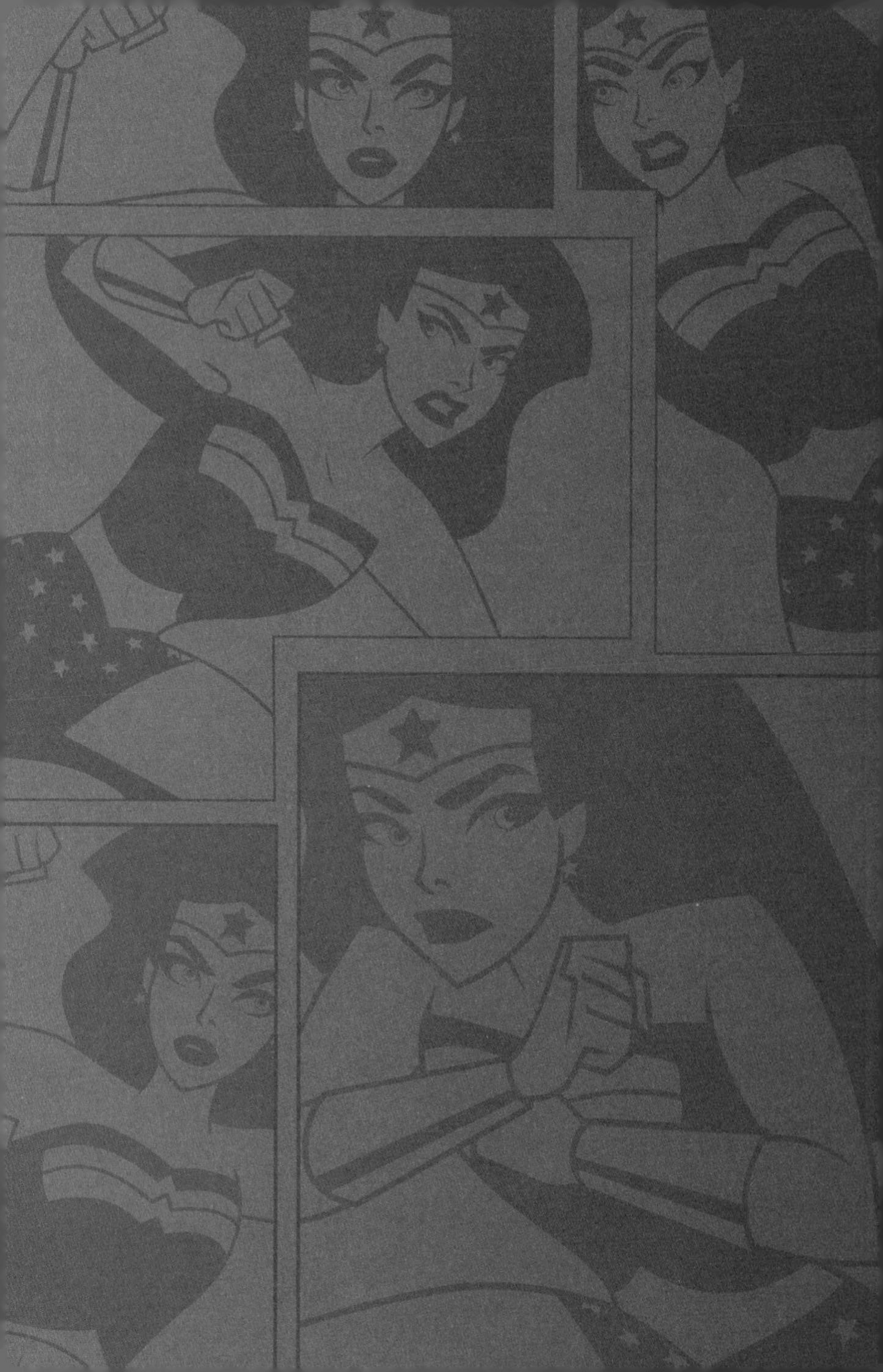

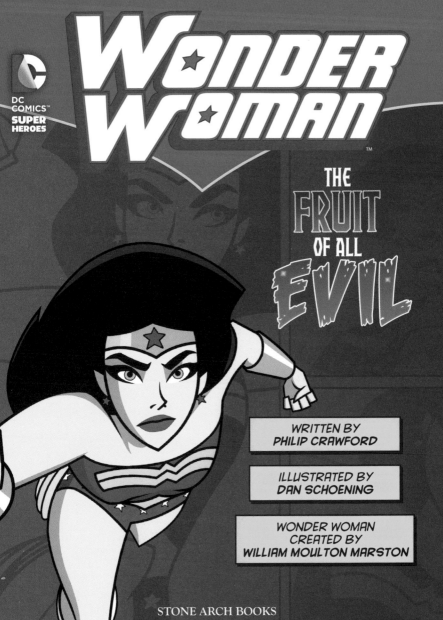

DC COMICS™
SUPER HEROES

WONDER WOMAN™

THE FRUIT OF ALL EVIL

WRITTEN BY
PHILIP CRAWFORD

ILLUSTRATED BY
DAN SCHOENING

WONDER WOMAN
CREATED BY
WILLIAM MOULTON MARSTON

STONE ARCH BOOKS
a capstone imprint

Published by Stone Arch Books
A Capstone Imprint
1710 Roe Crest Drive
North Mankato, Minnesota 56003
www.capstonepub.com

STAR13270

Cataloging-in-Publication Data is available on the Library of Congress
website.

ISBN: 978-1-4342-2017-2 (library binding)
ISBN: 978-1-4342-2766-9 (paperback)

Summary: During an amateur baseball game in Washington, D.C., a young
girl tosses a strange, glowing apple onto the field. Suddenly, the players
and fans become angry and turn violent. In the center of the chaos, a fire
erupts, and Ares, the God of War, emerges from the flames. His daughter,
Eris, has created enough anger with her golden apple to refuel her father's
superpowers. But when Eris is wounded, Ares must strike a deal with
Wonder Woman. Save his daughter, or he will destroy the world.

Art Director: Bob Lentz
Designer: Kay Fraser

Printed in the United States of America in Stevens Point, Wisconsin.
112013
007879R

TABLE OF CONTENTS

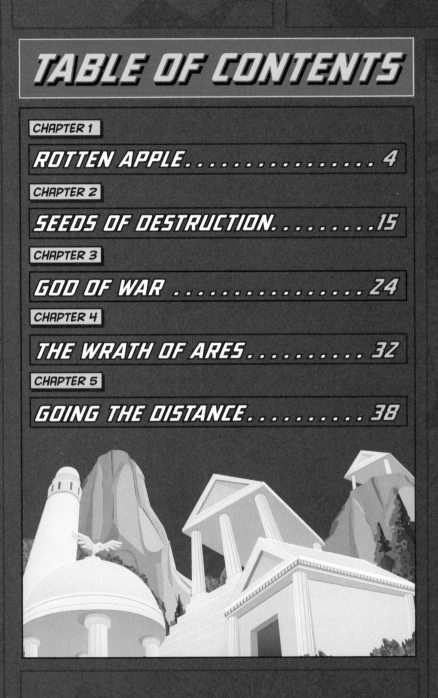

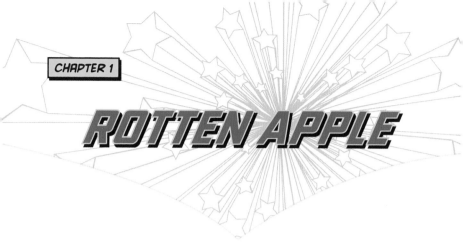

CHAPTER 1

ROTTEN APPLE

Trevor Barnes, peace advocate for the United Nations, walked through a park in Washington, D.C. He was there to watch an amateur baseball game and take in the beautiful summer day.

When he got to the field, Trevor went straight for the snack stand. He ordered a hot dog with mustard, onion and relish, and a soda — his favorite meal. In fact, the only thing Trevor liked more than hot dogs was baseball. And today, he was excited to have a heaping helping of both.

The bleachers were packed with fans, so Trevor found a seat near the top row. He sat down, took a bite of his hot dog, and grinned widely.

"This is a perfect way to spend a Sunday!" Trevor said to himself.

As he ate, Trevor noticed a little blonde girl with pigtails walk up the bleacher steps. *There's something strange about that girl,* thought Trevor. Her eyes looked like glowing rubies. He was trying to remember where he had seen her when the game suddenly began.

"Play ball!" yelled the umpire.

The audience cheered as the batter stepped up to the plate. Trevor turned his attention to the game. Soon, he had forgotten all about the strange child.

The pitcher nodded his head and began his windup. The ball sailed toward home. The batter choked up on the bat and swung, but the ball shot right past him.

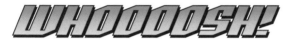

"Strike one!" the umpire yelled.

The batter stood over home plate and readied himself for the next pitch. As it crossed the plate, he swung with all his might.

The ball shot straight up into the air. It began to fall toward the stands, right where Trevor was sitting. He stood to catch the ball, but the little girl ran up to him and kicked him in the shins.

"Oww!" Trevor howled.

Before he could stop her, the girl leaped in front of him and snagged the baseball.

"I got it! I got it!" the girl shouted.

"Why did you kick me?" asked Trevor.

"I wanted the ball, and you were in my way," she replied. "Finders keepers, losers weepers!" The girl stuck out her tongue.

Trevor stood there, silent and stunned. He watched as the rude girl skipped back to her seat. As she sat there playing with the ball, the pitcher called from the field.

"Hey, can we have the ball back?" asked the player. "We only have a few left."

The girl ignored him and kept playing with the ball. The team grew restless.

"Come on, kid, we need that ball," shouted the first baseman.

"Stop whining!" the girl replied. "I'll give you back your dumb ball."

As the girl lifted her arm to throw the ball back, a strange red glow formed around her hand. "Here you go, you big babies!" she screamed.

THUD! The ball landed at the pitcher's feet. He bent down to pick it up, but was surprised at what he saw. The ball had transformed into a solid gold orb.

"What's the holdup?" the coach yelled.

The pitcher scratched his head. "The ball changed into a, um, golden apple," said the confused pitcher.

Suddenly, the catcher's eyes flashed a bright red. "It's mine!" he said.

The catcher threw down his glove and ran toward the pitcher's mound. When he reached the pitcher, he snatched the golden apple and ran.

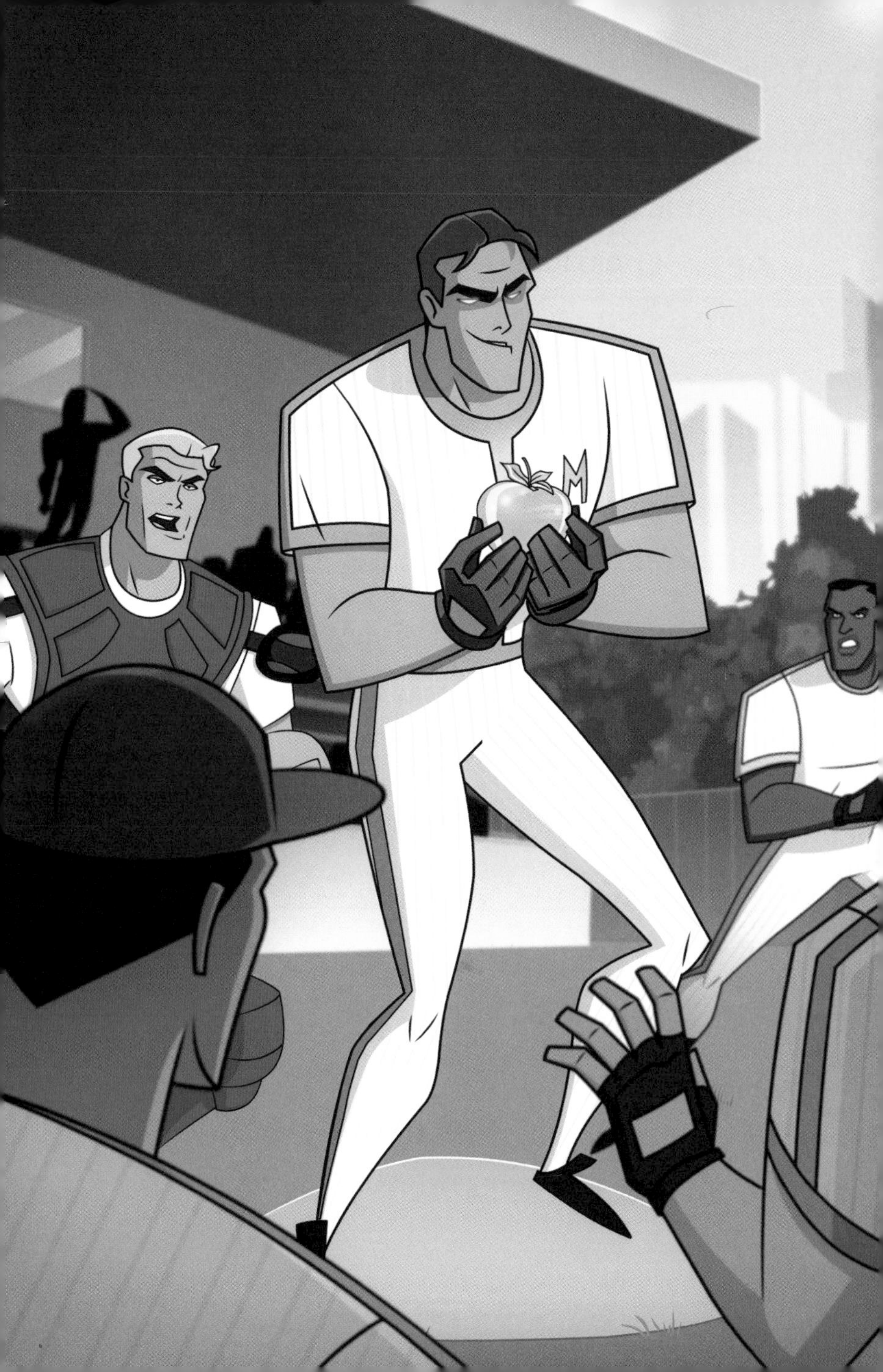

"Hey!" yelled the pitcher. He ran up to the catcher, but the man just dangled the heavy apple over his head and laughed at his teammate.

"Give me that thing!" the pitcher demanded. He pushed the other man hard. The catcher dropped the golden apple, and the two men began fighting over it.

"Hey, break it up!" shouted the coach. He yanked the players apart. "What's gotten into you two?"

Suddenly, the apple at their feet began to glow. Three snakes with red, glowing eyes sprouted out of its sides.

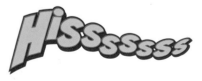

"Move away!" shouted the coach. He spread his arms to protect his players.

The team watched in horror as the serpents lifted their heads. Beams of red light shot from their eyes.

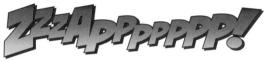

The rays swept across the stands, covering the bleachers in an eerie glow.

As the rays came toward Trevor, he ducked just in time to miss them. When the rays passed, he stood up and looked around. Everyone was fighting, except the little girl. She stood at the top of the bleachers like a conductor standing in front of an orchestra.

"What have you done?" Trevor asked.

The little girl turned around and looked at Trevor. He gasped when he saw her face. Her eyes were glowing. As she stared at Trevor, her lips curled into an evil grin.

"Nice to see you again, Trevor," she said.

"How do you know my name?" he asked. "I've never seen you before."

"Oh, but you have, Mr. Barnes," she said. "Ask your friend Wonder Woman." She tossed back her head and laughed. Then she turned and ran down the steps.

"Wait! Who are you?" Trevor demanded as he hurried after the girl.

As she ran into a crowded area, the girl shot red rays at the people she passed.

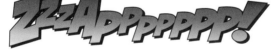

Each person she struck quickly became violent. As Trevor made his way through the angry mob, he lost sight of the little girl. He stopped and looked around. She was nowhere to be seen. The crowd was out of control, just like at the ballpark.

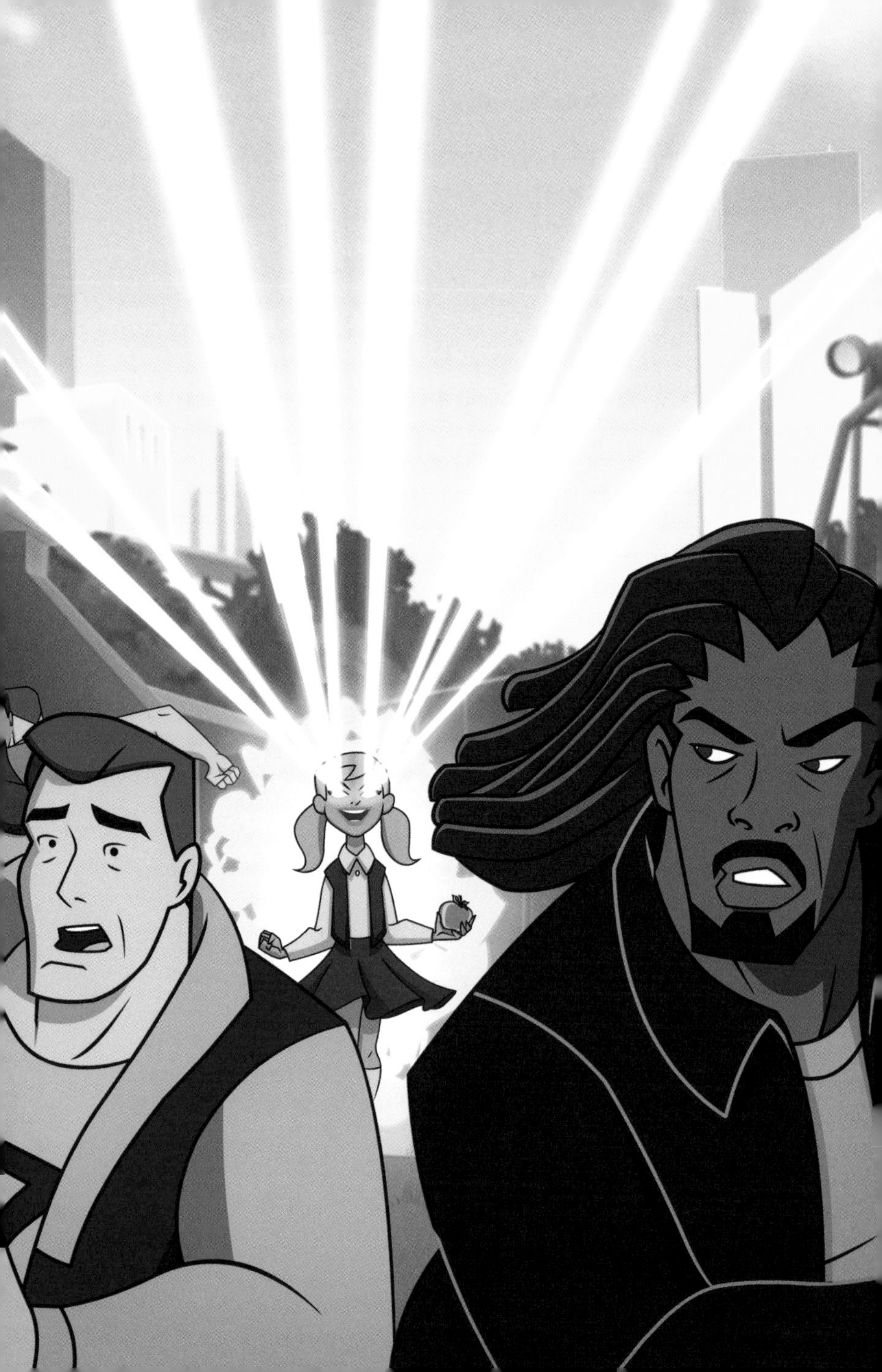

Trevor had no way of stopping the angry mob, but he knew one person who could. *I'd better contact Wonder Woman before this gets even more out of hand,* he thought.

Trevor slipped through the crowd and ducked behind an empty park bench. He grabbed his cell phone from his pocket and punched in a text message. Just as he hit Send, the golden apple shot over the bench and struck him in the back of his head.

KRAK! The heavy blow knocked him unconscious.

A shadow fell over him. The girl picked up the golden apple. "That's strike three," she said. "You're out!"

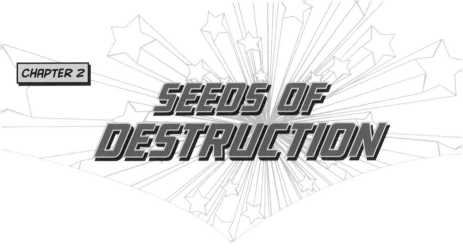

CHAPTER 2

SEEDS OF DESTRUCTION

Wonder Woman was returning from Themyscira in her Invisible Jet when she got the message. An alarm sounded on her plane's computer. When she looked down at the monitor, the words "WW – HELP – URGENT – TB" flashed across the screen. She knew it was from Trevor. He was one of the few people who had access to her jet's communication system.

Wonder Woman pressed a green button on the navigation panel. "Computer, locate Trevor Barnes," she commanded.

BEEP! BEEP! BEEP!

The computer beeped several times as it searched for her friend. When it found him, a map appeared on the screen. Wonder Woman looked down at the flashing arrow. It was pointed at Washington, D.C.

"Computer, switch to camera," she said. "I need to see what's going on down there."

Wonder Woman watched as the computer displayed the riots on the screen. She flipped a switch and set the plane to autopilot. The jet swerved sharply to the left and then kicked into high speed.

ZWWWOOOOMMMM!

Wonder Woman held on tight as the plane zoomed toward the park. In seconds, it was above the field. She set the controls to hover, opened the hatch, and leaped out.

Speeding toward the ground, Wonder Woman quickly spotted Trevor and raced to his side. He was just beginning to wake up.

"Wonder Woman! I'm so glad you're here," Trevor said. He tried to stand up but fell right back down. He was still dizzy from the blow to his head.

Wonder Woman looked down at her friend with concern. "Trevor, what's going on here?" she asked.

"I don't remember. All of a sudden everybody started going crazy," he said.

"Focus, Trevor. I need you to remember what happened," said Wonder Woman.

Trevor closed his eyes and retraced the events of the day. He told Wonder Woman about the little girl, the golden apple, and the snakes with glowing eyes.

"Trevor, I must find that girl," said Wonder Woman. "Do you remember where she went?"

Trevor thought for a moment and then pointed to the left. "That way," he said.

"You can rest now," she said. "I'll bring you to my Invisible Jet for safekeeping."

Wonder Woman quickly flew Trevor to her jet in the sky. Once he was safe inside, she soared over the park and searched for the girl. A moment later, she spotted the child by the concession stand.

"Stop!" Wonder Woman commanded.

The girl kept running. Wonder Woman pulled her Golden Lasso and twirled it in the air. The rope landed around the girl's shoulders. Wonder Woman yanked on the lasso as she swooped down from the sky.

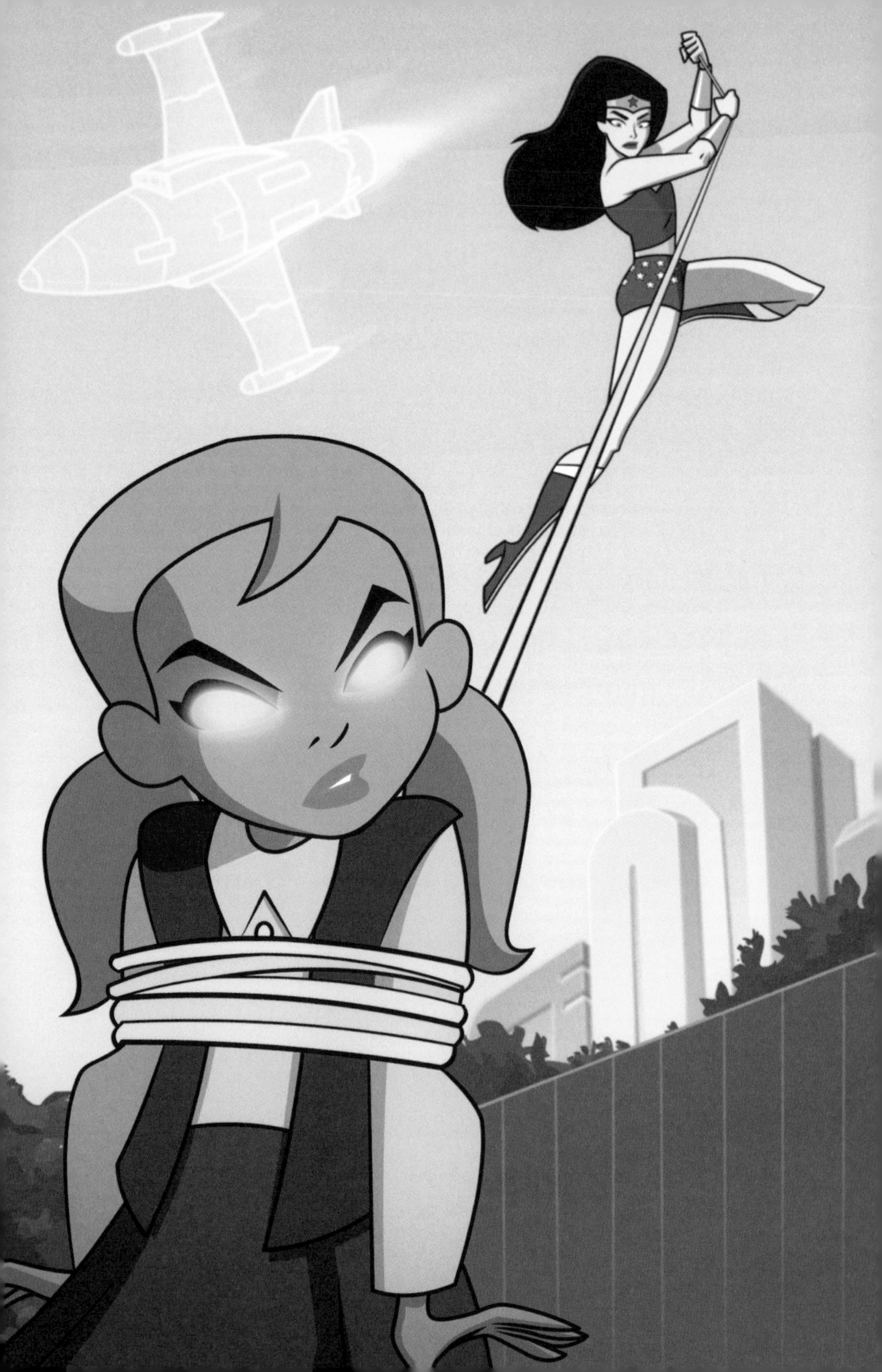

"Don't fight it," Wonder Woman said. "Anyone bound by my unbreakable lasso must tell the truth. Now who are you?"

The girl looked at Wonder Woman and laughed. "Don't you recognize me, foolish Amazon?" she asked.

Wonder Woman watched as a circle of flames shot up around the girl. The super hero released her grip as a cloud of red smoke swallowed the girl up. A moment later, a woman emerged wearing a suit of armor. Her eyes were red with fire.

"Do you recognize me now, Wonder Woman?" she said, laughing.

"Eris!" Wonder Woman exclaimed, identifying the Goddess of Discord. "I should have known it was you. Anyone touched by your rays becomes violent."

"And you're next," shouted Eris.

The evil goddess pointed toward Wonder Woman. A yellow ball of energy formed in her hand. **BZZZT!**

She hurled it at Wonder Woman. The Amazon's fists moved in a blinding flash as she deflected the ball with her sliver bracelets. **CHING! CHING!**

Wonder Woman jumped at Eris and leveled her with one blow. **CRUNCH!**

She reached down and grabbed Eris by the collar and yanked her up. Wonder Woman looked directly into her eyes.

"Why are you here?" asked the super hero. "I'm tired of playing these games."

"Turn around and find out," replied Eris. A huge cloud of black smoke sprung up on the field. "The guest of honor just arrived!"

As Wonder Woman turned around, a tall, angry figure stepped out of the black cloud. His broad shoulders and massive chest were covered in dark armor. He stood nearly ten feet tall. His evil laughter echoed in Wonder Woman's ears.

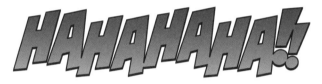

"It can't be!" Wonder Woman cried out.

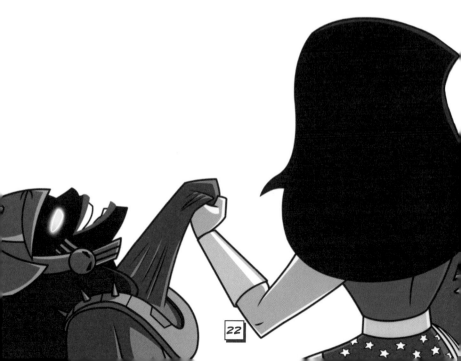

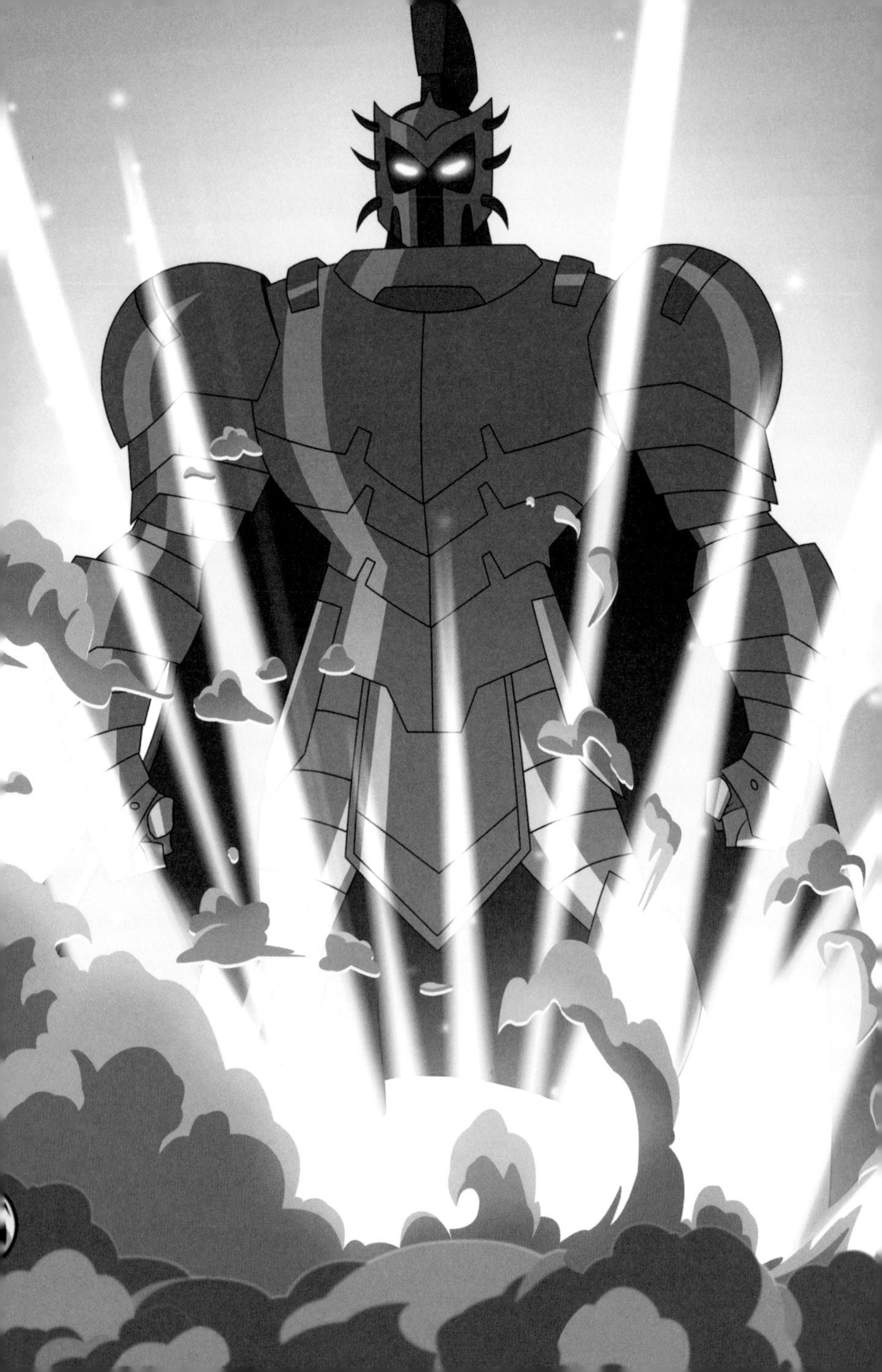

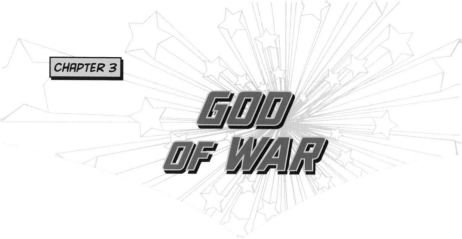

CHAPTER 3

GOD OF WAR

Wonder Woman stared in amazement at the figure who stood in front of her. "What evil released you from your prison, Ares?" Wonder Woman shouted.

The God of War put his arm around Eris and smiled at her. "Like father, like daughter," he said with a smile.

Eris stepped toward Wonder Woman, holding the golden apple in her hand. "My father's energy grows stronger with every conflict I create," she said. "It's like food to him!"

"My daughter is right," Ares added. "The chaos Eris created today gave me enough strength to break free."

Ares lifted his hands above his head. In each fist, a ball of lava smoldered. "And now, I'm going to break *you*!" he shouted.

Before Ares had a chance to attack, Wonder Woman clenched her fists and put her arms out like a battering ram. Using her super-speed, she slammed into the war god's chest. **WHAM!** The blow was so powerful it knocked him to the ground.

When Ares got up, he was furious. "No one makes a fool of me!" he yelled. **SMASH!** He crushed the fireballs in his hands, changing them into a handful of glowing coals. "Take this!" he said, throwing the hot stones at Wonder Woman.

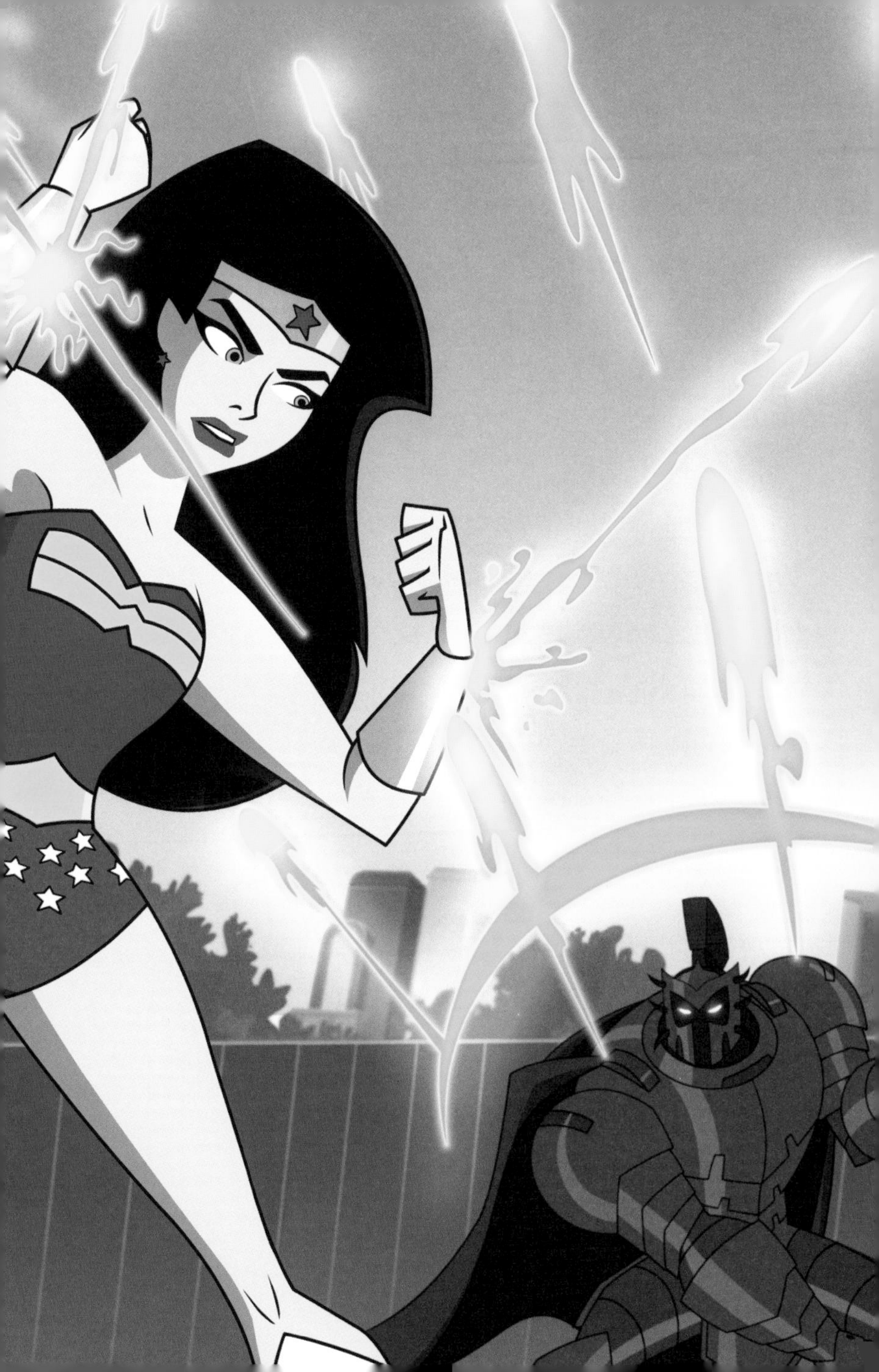

Wonder Woman held up her fists. Her arms blurred with speed. As the coals flew toward her, she deflected them one by one.

CHING! CLANK! CHING!

As the two battled, Eris raced to the nearby Potomac River. She soared over the city, firing her evil rays at the people below. Within minutes, nearly the entire city had turned into an angry mob.

When Eris reached the river, she swerved toward a U.S. Navy ship anchored along the shoreline. She aimed her ray at the captain as she flew over.

As his eyes filled with rage, he spotted the button on the control panel that read "Missile Launch." The captain reached across the flashing lights and pressed the button. The missile shot into the sky.

The fight between Wonder Woman and Ares was in full force when the missile was released.

"I've had enough of your games, Ares," Wonder Woman said.

The Amazon Princess flew into the sky, speeding past Ares' head in a streak of red, blue, and gold. She somersaulted in midair and shot back down toward Ares. Wonder Woman slammed into the back of the war god's head, feet first. The blow knocked Ares to his knees.

Wasting no time, the super hero grabbed her Golden Lasso and swung it toward Ares. As the rope sailed through the air, the missile suddenly streaked across the sky.

WHOOOOSH!

A gust of wind from the missile blew Wonder Woman's lasso off course. It missed Ares and fell to the ground.

At the same time, the Amazon Princess looked over her shoulder and cried out in horror. "There's a missile headed straight for the Washington Monument!" she exclaimed.

"Hahaha!" Ares shouted. "Eris must be celebrating my return with some fireworks!"

"If that missile hits the city, thousands will die!" Wonder Woman said.

She shot into the air, racing after the missile with lighting speed. The missile was soaring over the Washington Monument when she finally reached it. Without a moment to lose, Wonder Woman grabbed for her lasso.

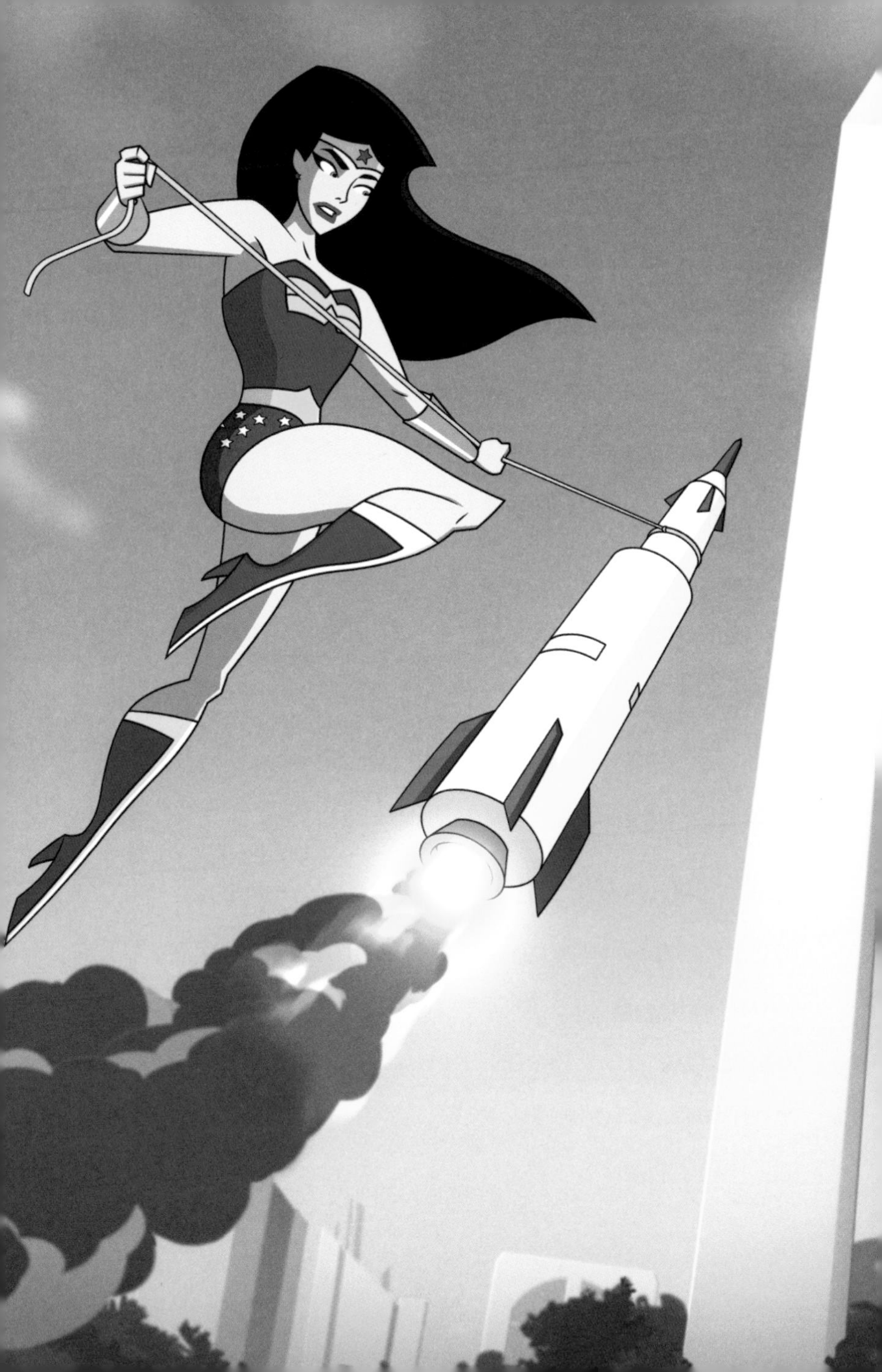

Using her Golden Lasso, the Amazon Princess caught the missile. She pulled it off course only seconds before it could hit the famous tower. Then she spun the missile around like a sling and released it into the air.

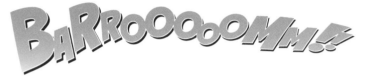

It exploded harmlessly in outer space.

Now that the threat was over, Wonder Woman raced back to Earth. When she returned, Ares had not moved — but he had changed. He was taller and stronger, having grown more powerful from the chaos Eris had created.

"Back for more, Wonder Woman?" he said with a laugh. "This time, I'll show you what it means to be the God of War!"

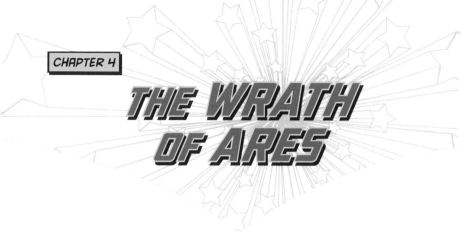

CHAPTER 4

THE WRATH OF ARES

Ares stared down at Wonder Woman. "I am ten times stronger than I was before," he said, hovering above the super hero. "Are you afraid, Princess?"

Wonder Woman stood her ground. "I am an Amazon warrior," she said, holding up her fists. "I fear no man!"

Ares raised his arms above his head. **BZZZT!** Bolts of lightning crackled between his hands. He howled as the energy grew more and more powerful.

While Ares prepared to strike, Eris landed quietly on the grass behind Wonder Woman. She crept up to the super hero.

Suddenly, Ares fired a thousand volts of electricity directly at the Amazon Princess. Wonder Woman was ready for the blast. She leaped out of the way, and the lightning whizzed past her. **BZZZT!**

"Ugh!" Eris screamed as the deadly bolts struck and knocked her to the ground.

"What have I done?" Ares shouted. He ran to his daughter's side and held her in his arms. "I never meant to harm you."

Eris looked up at her father. "Please help me," she said. Her voice was weak. "I feel the life force draining from my body."

"I may be a god, but I don't have the power to heal," Ares replied.

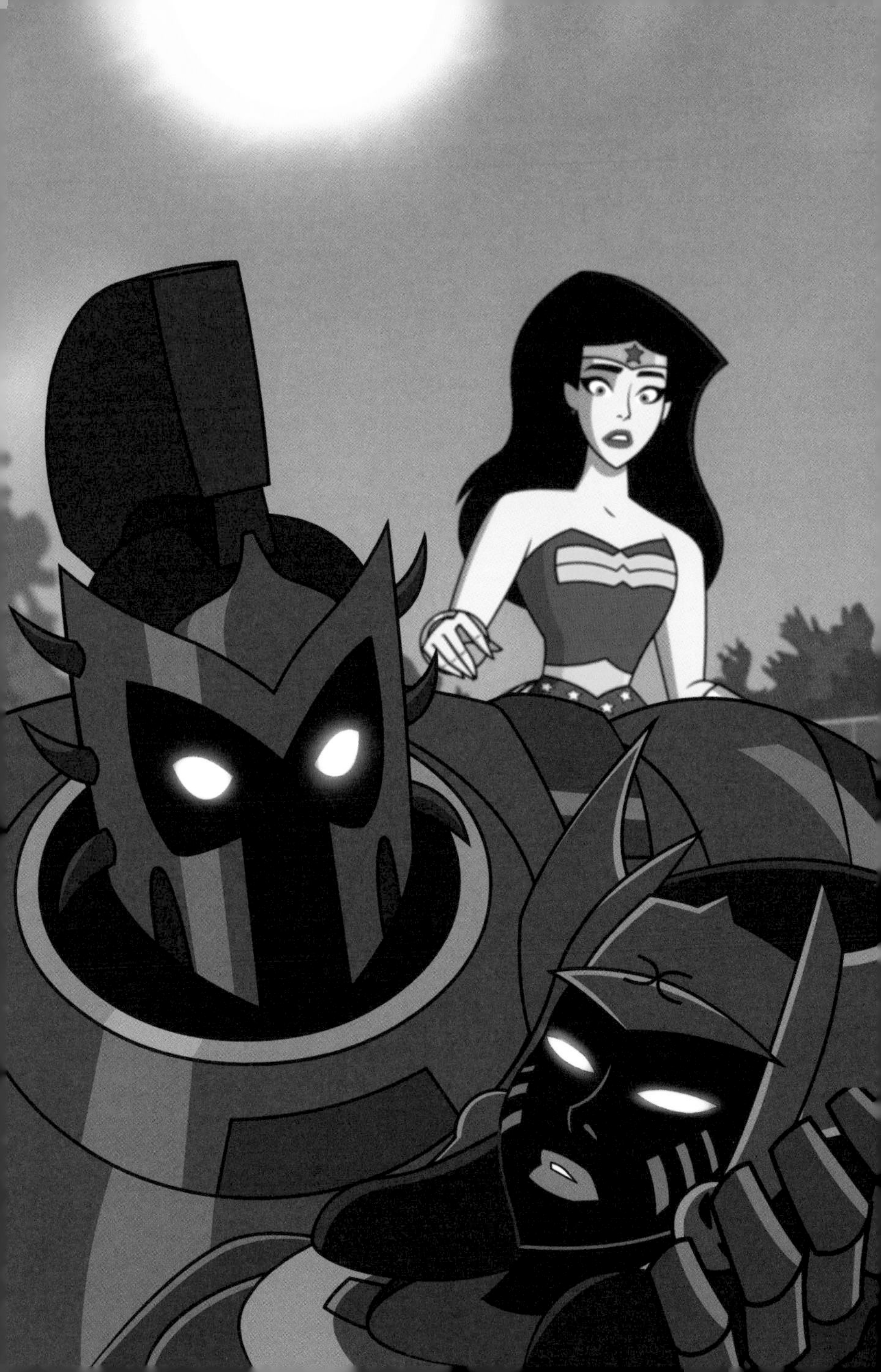

Eris fell unconscious in her father's arms. Ares slowly lowered her to the grass. Then he stood and turned to confront Wonder Woman. The hate and rage in his eyes was monstrous as he stomped toward her.

"This is your fault, Amazon!" Ares shouted. "If my daughter dies, I will destroy the entire human race!"

"I can save her," said Wonder Woman.

"You know nothing of healing!" Ares said.

"You're right," she said. "But I know someone who does."

"Then tell me who, or I'll crush you into dust!" Ares threatened.

"I will take her to Themyscira," said Wonder Woman. "Our chief healer, Epione, can save her with the Purple Healing Ray."

Ares paused. "So be it," he finally said.

A moment later, the Invisible Jet landed next to the super hero. Wonder Woman walked over to Eris and lifted her gently.

"Not so fast," Ares said. Suddenly, a giant hourglass appeared in his hand. He turned it upside down, and a thin stream of sand flowed toward the bottom.

Ares pointed to the hourglass and smirked. "Make haste, Amazon," he said. "You have less than three hours to save my daughter. If you fail, I will destroy you and everyone else on this miserable planet!"

Wonder Woman nodded at the God of War. "I will not fail," she said.

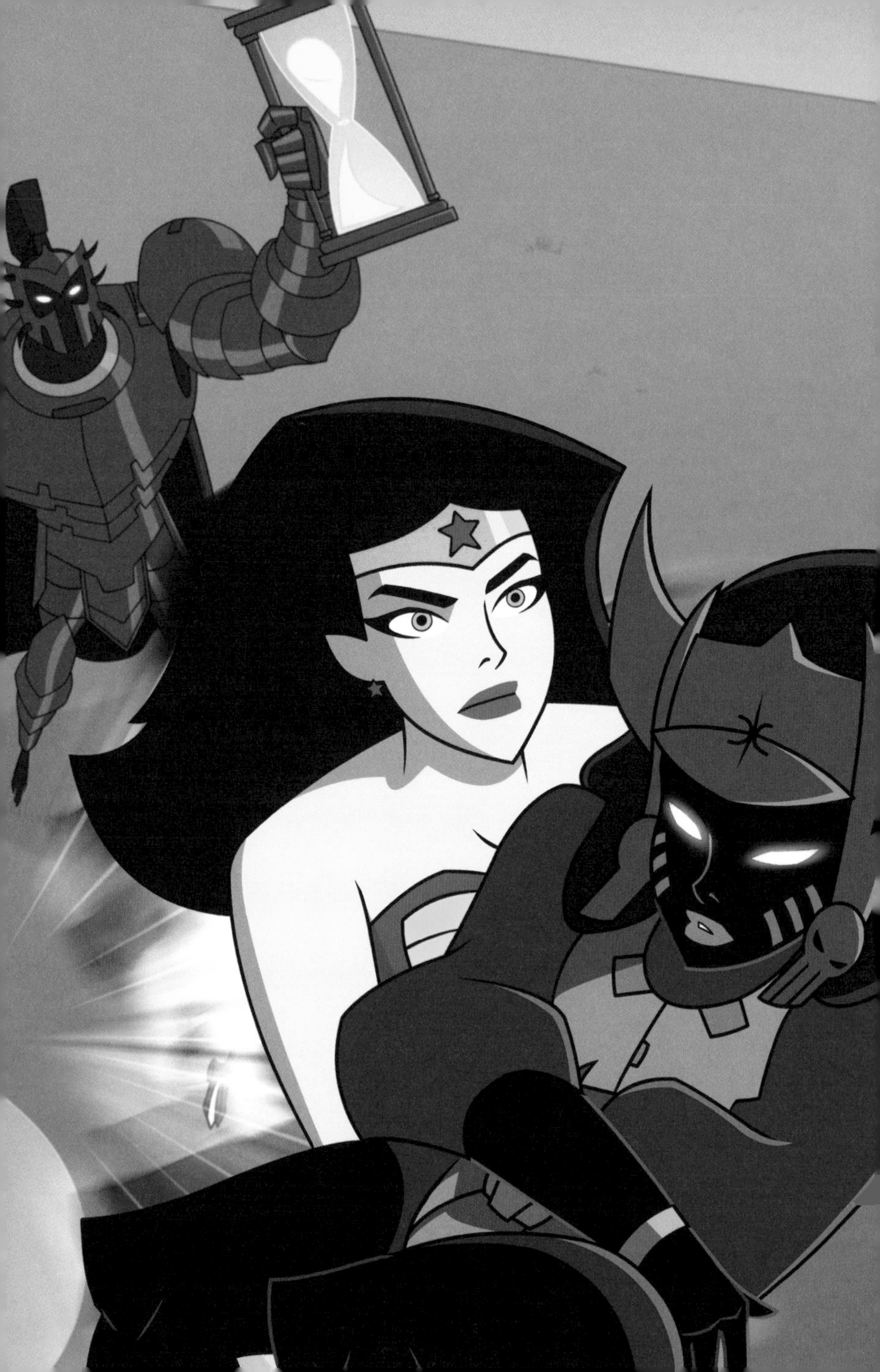

CHAPTER 5

GOING THE DISTANCE

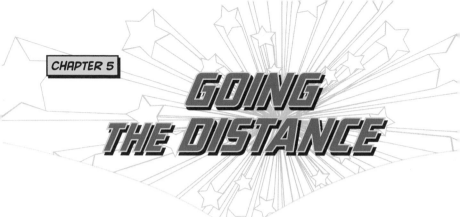

zWWWWOOOOMMMM!

The Invisible Jet flew toward Themyscira, the home of the Amazons. Inside, Wonder Woman strapped Eris onto a cot.

"How are you feeling?" Wonder Woman asked Trevor, who was lying nearby.

Trevor looked up at Wonder Woman and smiled. "Better, but my head still aches," he replied. Then he pointed toward the Goddess of Discord, not recognizing her in adult form. "Who is she?"

"That's Eris," replied Wonder Woman, "the daughter of the God of War. I'm taking her to the Healing Center on Themyscira." She put her hand on Trevor's shoulder and smiled at her injured friend. "Don't worry, Trevor. I will get help for you too. I only hope we get there in time to save Eris."

Wonder Woman stood up and headed toward the pilot's seat. She switched on her communication system and contacted her mother, Queen Hippolyta.

The queen's face appeared on the display screen. Wonder Woman's face lit up. "Mother, I need your help!" exclaimed Wonder Woman. "Eris is on the brink of death, and we must save her."

"Save Eris?" asked the Queen. "But why? She is our sworn enemy."

"Please, Mother, we don't have a moment to lose," replied Wonder Woman. "If Eris dies, Ares will destroy Earth!"

"Then I'll meet you at the shore when you land," said the queen, no longer questioning her daughter's urgency.

The display screen went black as the jet continued toward the home of the Amazons. When the plane landed a few moments later, Queen Hippolyta was accompanied by the great warrior, Artemis. Phillipus, the queen's general and chief advisor, was also by her side.

The three Amazons watched as the jet's hatch flew open, and Wonder Woman poked her head out. "Artemis! Phillipus!" the super hero called to her friends. "Bring Eris to the Healing Center! We haven't a moment to lose."

"Stay here, Trevor," Wonder Woman said. "I'll return with someone to help you." Trevor nodded and fell back to sleep.

As Wonder Woman stepped from the plane, her mother ran toward her. The queen hugged her daughter while the two powerful warriors rushed toward the Healing Center with Eris.

Hippolyta took her daughter by the hand. "Come," she commanded. "We must discuss how to defeat Ares."

The queen walked with Wonder Woman by her side. "The God of War feeds off of his daughter's conflicts," began the queen. "In order to weaken and capture Ares, you must first stop the chaos on Earth."

"But how?" asked Wonder Woman. "Too many people have already been affected."

"Stop the origin of the virus," the queen continued, "and the infection will end."

Wonder Woman looked at her mother and smiled. "I have a plan," she said.

A short time later, the chief healer, Epione, returned with Eris. "It is done, your Highness," she said to the queen. "Eris still needs plenty of rest to fully recover, and so does the man in the plane."

"The world thanks you," said the Amazon Princess.

As Wonder Woman spoke, Eris began to rise from her stretcher, but she was still very weak. "What am I doing here?" she demanded. "Where is my father?"

"You are on Themyscira," said Wonder Woman. "This is Epione, our chief healer. She is the doctor who saved your life."

"I don't care who she is!" Eris shrieked. "Take me back at once!" Exhausted, Eris settled back down and closed her eyes.

When everyone was in the plane, Wonder Woman steered the aircraft toward the park. A few moments later, the Invisible Jet set down in Washington, D.C. Wonder Woman opened the plane's door and raced toward Ares. The hourglass beside him was almost empty.

"I've returned, Ares," said Wonder Woman. "Your daughter is weak, but she will recover."

He looked at the plane and watched as Trevor helped Eris climb out of the jet. "So, you succeeded, Wonder Woman," he said, pointing at the hourglass. The last grains had just fallen to the bottom. "And just in the nick of time!"

Ares walked past Wonder Woman toward his daughter. "Welcome back, daughter," he said. "As soon as you are well, we will continue our plan to take over the world!"

"I knew you couldn't be trusted," Wonder Woman said.

"Did you expect that the God of War would speak the truth?" Ares howled with laughter. "You are a fool, Amazon!"

Knowing she only had a split second before they would be gone, Wonder Woman grabbed her Golden Lasso and threw it through the air. **WHOOOOSH!** She snared Ares easily.

While he struggled, Hippolyta, Artemis, and Phillipus jumped out of the Invisible Jet, surprising Ares and his daughter.

Hippolyta and Artemis surrounded the God of War. At the same time, Phillipus ran to the nearby baseball field.

"Over there!" Wonder Woman shouted toward the queen's general.

Suddenly, Phillipus spotted the golden apple, glowing near the pitcher's mound. Trevor had told Wonder Woman about the evil fruit. She knew Eris had used the apple to start her chaos and destruction. It was also the only way to stop it.

"Now!" shouted Wonder Woman.

Phillipus picked up the golden apple. "Batter's up!" she said, winding up and hurling it toward the Amazon Princess.

Still holding Ares in her Golden Lasso, Wonder Woman watched the apple streak toward her like a fastball.

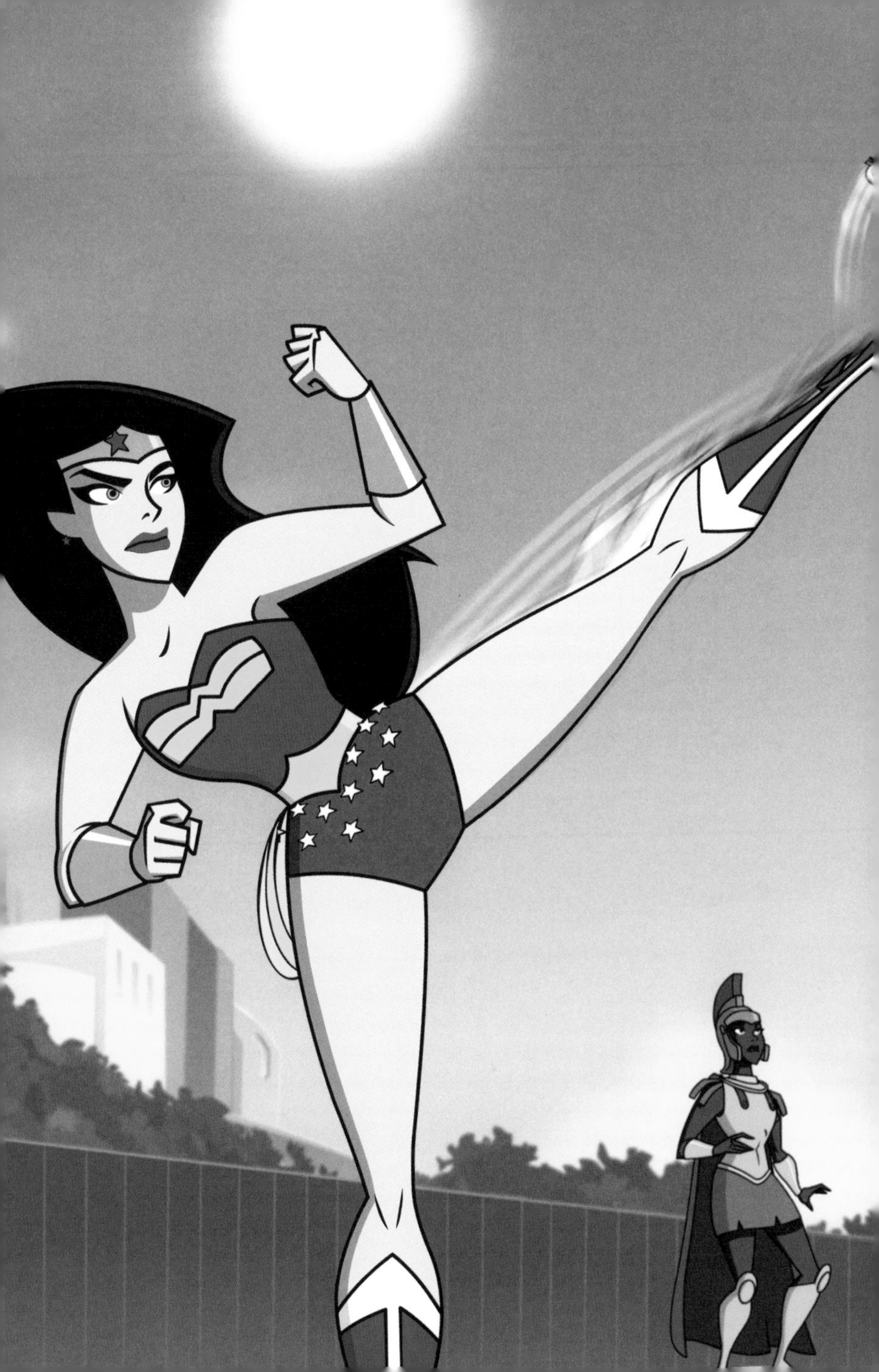

Just before the evil fruit reached her, Wonder Woman swung her leg. **KRAK!** She kicked the evil apple with all her might. It soared out of the ballpark and through the earth's atmosphere.

AAAAAHHH! Ares screamed. As the golden apple disappeared, the crazed park visitors quickly returned to normal. All the power drained from the God of War's body.

"We're taking you back to Mount Olympus, Ares," said Queen Hippolyta. "Zeus has prepared a prison for both of you." The Amazons dragged Ares, kicking and growling, back to the Invisible Jet.

Moments later, the queen came back with Trevor. "Take care of him, Diana. But now that the apple is gone, he should be fine as well," she said. "I will send back the jet when we have Eris and Ares in prison."

Wonder Woman and Trevor waved good-bye as the Invisible Jet took off toward Mount Olympus, home of the gods.

"Two villains in one day. Now, that's what I call a double play," said Trevor with a smile.

"You know what they say," Wonder Woman replied. "Teamwork divides the task and doubles the success."

"Yeah," said Trevor, "and it doesn't hurt to have a super hero waiting on deck."

Wonder Woman and Trevor laughed together as the sun set over the nation's capital.

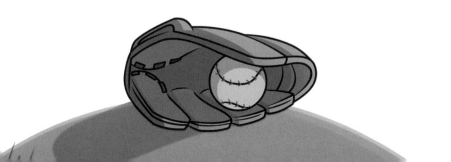

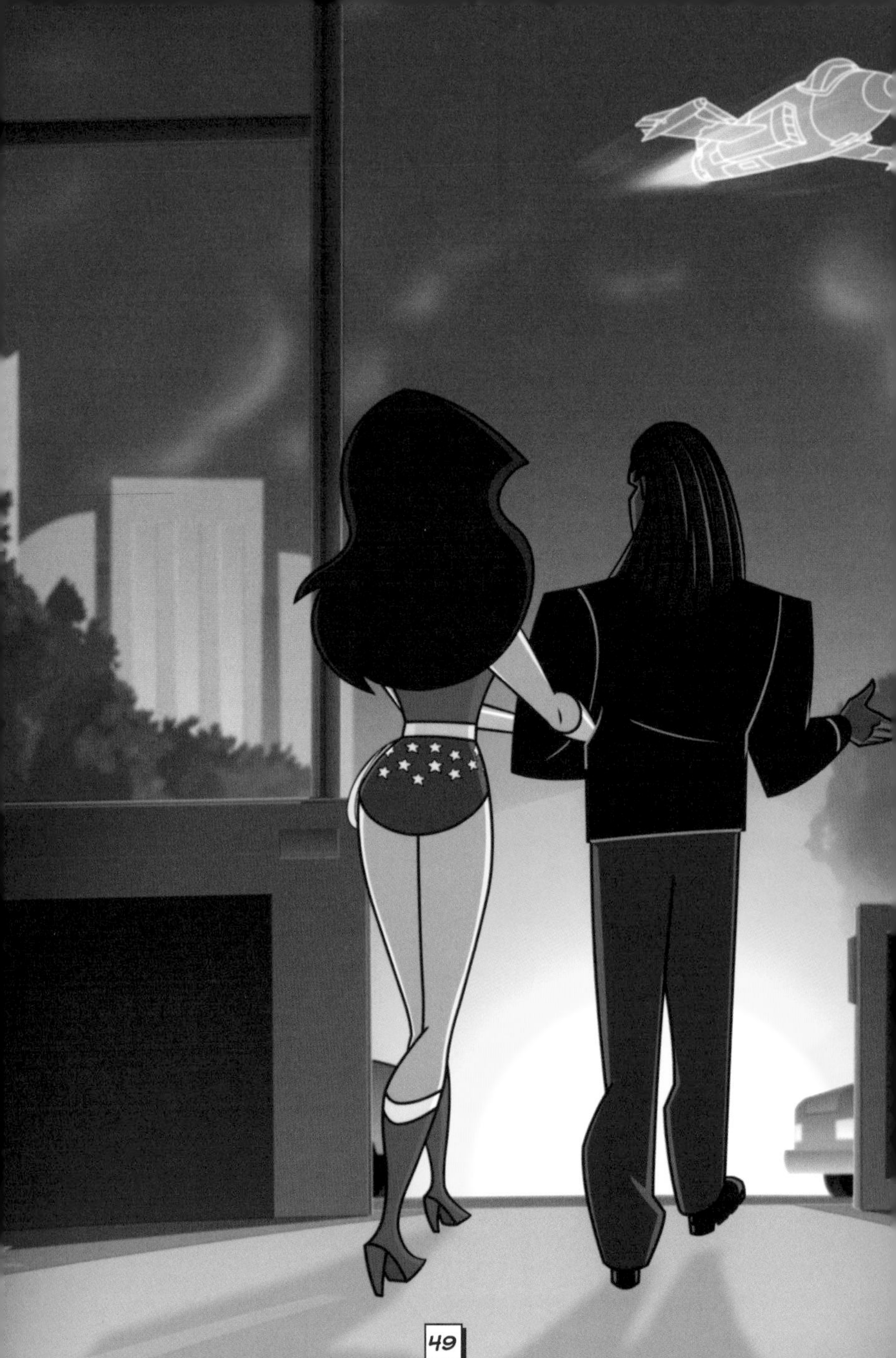

INVISIBLE PLANE
SECRET FILES

FILE NO. 3765 >>> ARES, GOD OF WAR

ENEMY ›› ALLY FRIEND

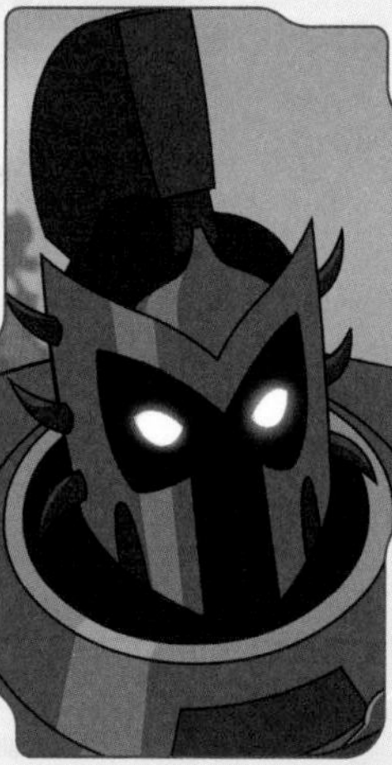

BASE: The Areopagus

OCCUPATION: God of War

HEIGHT: 6' 11" **WEIGHT:** 495 lbs

EYES: Red **HAIR:** Unknown

POWERS/ABILITIES: Immortality; unmatched strength and stamina; indestructible armor; military leader and strategist.

BIOGRAPHY

Although his father, Zeus, was King of the Gods, Ares never fit in on Mount Olympus. From an early age, he vowed to conquer Earth and overtake the human race. He left Olympus and created his own realm known as the Areopagus. While there, he began his destruction, creating chaos the world had never before seen. Thankfully, Earth had Wonder Woman on its side, born to stop Ares' threats of treachery and death.

CHILDREN OF ARES

The God of War has several children, each with their own evil powers:

Phobos, the God of Fear, can turn any nightmare into a reality.

Deimos, the God of Terror, has a beard of snakes, which bite with a panic-inducing venom.

Eris, the Goddess of Strife, may be the most powerful child of all. Just a bite — or even the sight — of her Golden Apples of Discord can fill the hearts of her victims with anger and hatred.

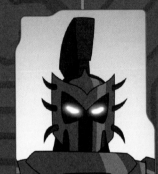

POWERS OF THE GODS

Ares might be the son of Zeus, but the Amazon Princess has the power of several goddesses:

· Demeter granted Wonder Woman her strength.

· Aphrodite gave her beauty and a loving heart.

· Athena allowed her to communicate with animals.

· Hermes granted her speed and the power of flight.

These superpowers make Woman Woman the God of War's most difficult enemy.

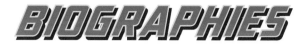

BIOGRAPHIES

Philip Crawford works as a high school librarian. He is the author of *Graphic Novels 101*, a resource guide for teachers and librarians. He is currently a graduate student in creative writing at Vermont College of Fine Arts. Philip lives in Vermont with his partner (also a writer) and their cat, Emily Pickles.

Dan Schoening was born in Victoria, B.C. Canada. From an early age, Dan has had a passion for animation and comic books. Currently, Dan does freelance work in the animation and game industry, and spends a lot of time with his lovely little daughter, Paige.

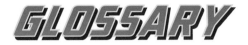

GLOSSARY

chaos (KAY-oss)—total confusion

conflict (KON-flict)—a war or period of fighting

discord (DISS-kord)—disagreement between two or more people

goddess (GOD-iss)—a female supernatural being who is worshipped

infection (in-FEK-shuhn)—an illness caused by germs or viruses

origin (OR-uh-jin)—the cause or source or something, or the point where something began

serpent (SUR-puhnt)—another name for a snake

smoldered (SMOHL-durd)—burned and smoked slowly with no flames

unconscious (uhn-KON-shuhss)—not awake, or unable to see, feel, or think

urgent (UR-juhnt)—in need of very quick or immediate attention

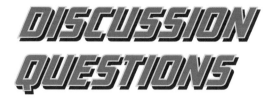

DISCUSSION QUESTIONS

1. Why did Wonder Woman choose to help Ares' evil daughter? Would you have made the same decision? Explain.

2. The Amazon Princess faces many challenges in this story. What is the toughest challenge you've ever overcome?

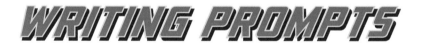

WRITING PROMPTS

1. In this story, Wonder Woman had to help both an ally and a villain. Have you ever had the same experience? Describe a time you helped a friend or an enemy.

2. If you could have one superpower, what would it be? Write a story about how you would use the ability.

3. Write your own Wonder Woman story. What villains will she battle? Which superpowers will she use to defeat them? You decide.

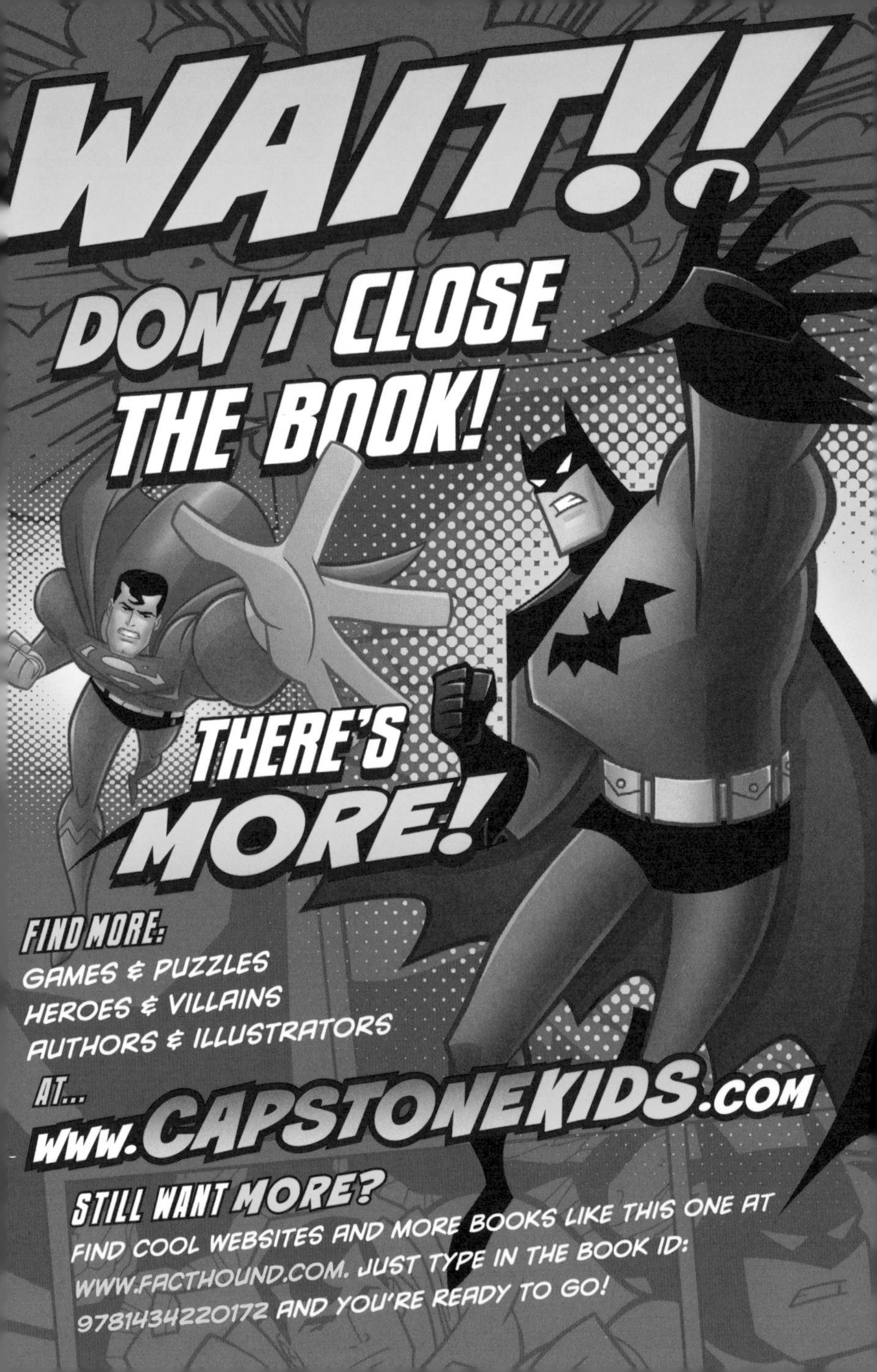
WAIT!!
DON'T CLOSE THE BOOK!
THERE'S MORE!
FIND MORE:
GAMES & PUZZLES
HEROES & VILLAINS
AUTHORS & ILLUSTRATORS
AT...
WWW.CAPSTONEKIDS.COM
STILL WANT MORE?
FIND COOL WEBSITES AND MORE BOOKS LIKE THIS ONE AT WWW.FACTHOUND.COM. JUST TYPE IN THE BOOK ID: 9781434220172 AND YOU'RE READY TO GO!

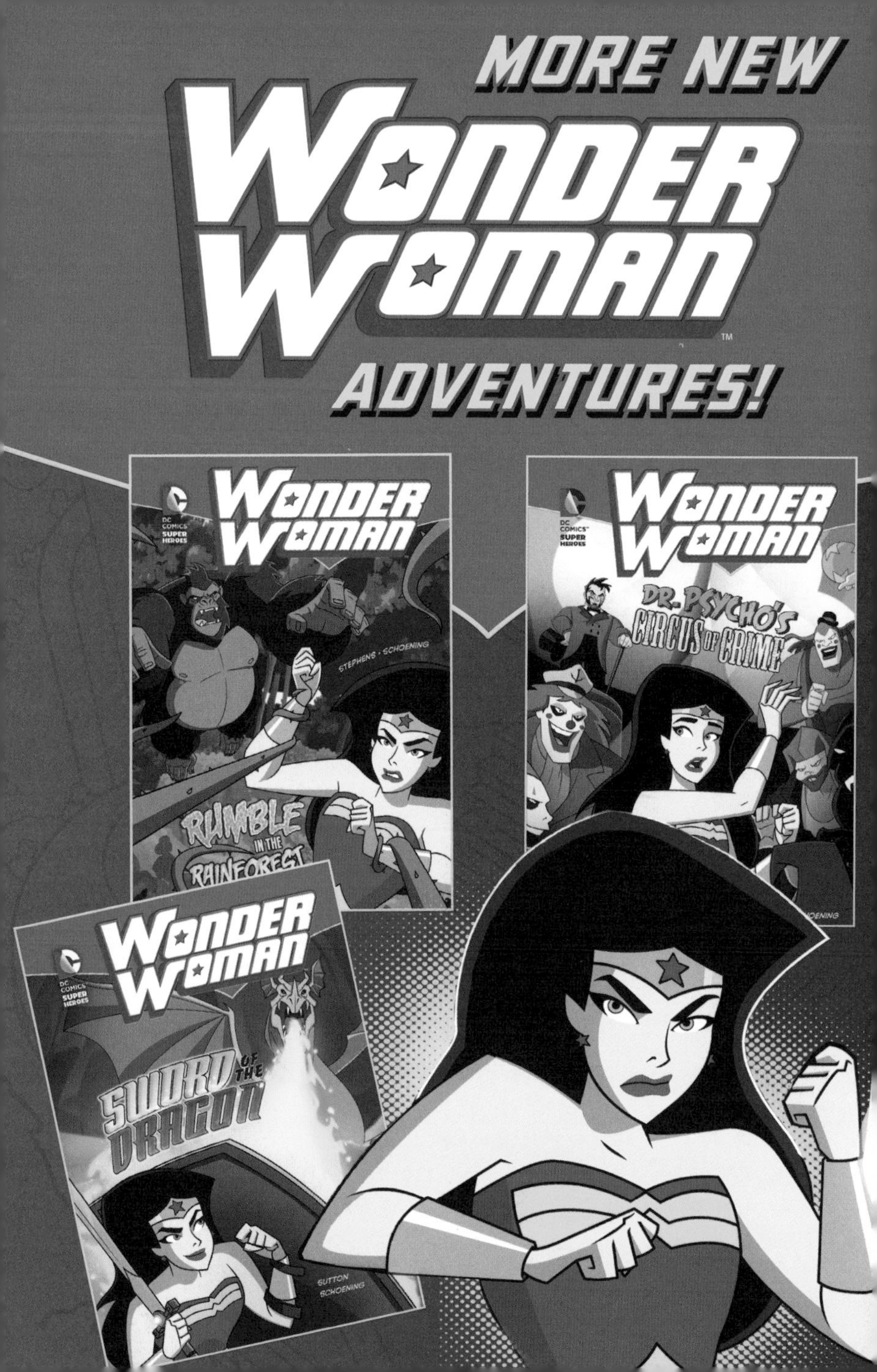
MORE NEW
WONDER WOMAN™
ADVENTURES!
WONDER WOMAN
DC COMICS SUPER HEROES
STEPHENS · SCHOENING
RUMBLE IN THE RAINFOREST
WONDER WOMAN
DC COMICS SUPER HEROES
DR. PSYCHO'S CIRCUS OF CRIME
WONDER WOMAN
DC COMICS SUPER HEROES
SWORD OF THE DRAGON
SUTTON
SCHOENING

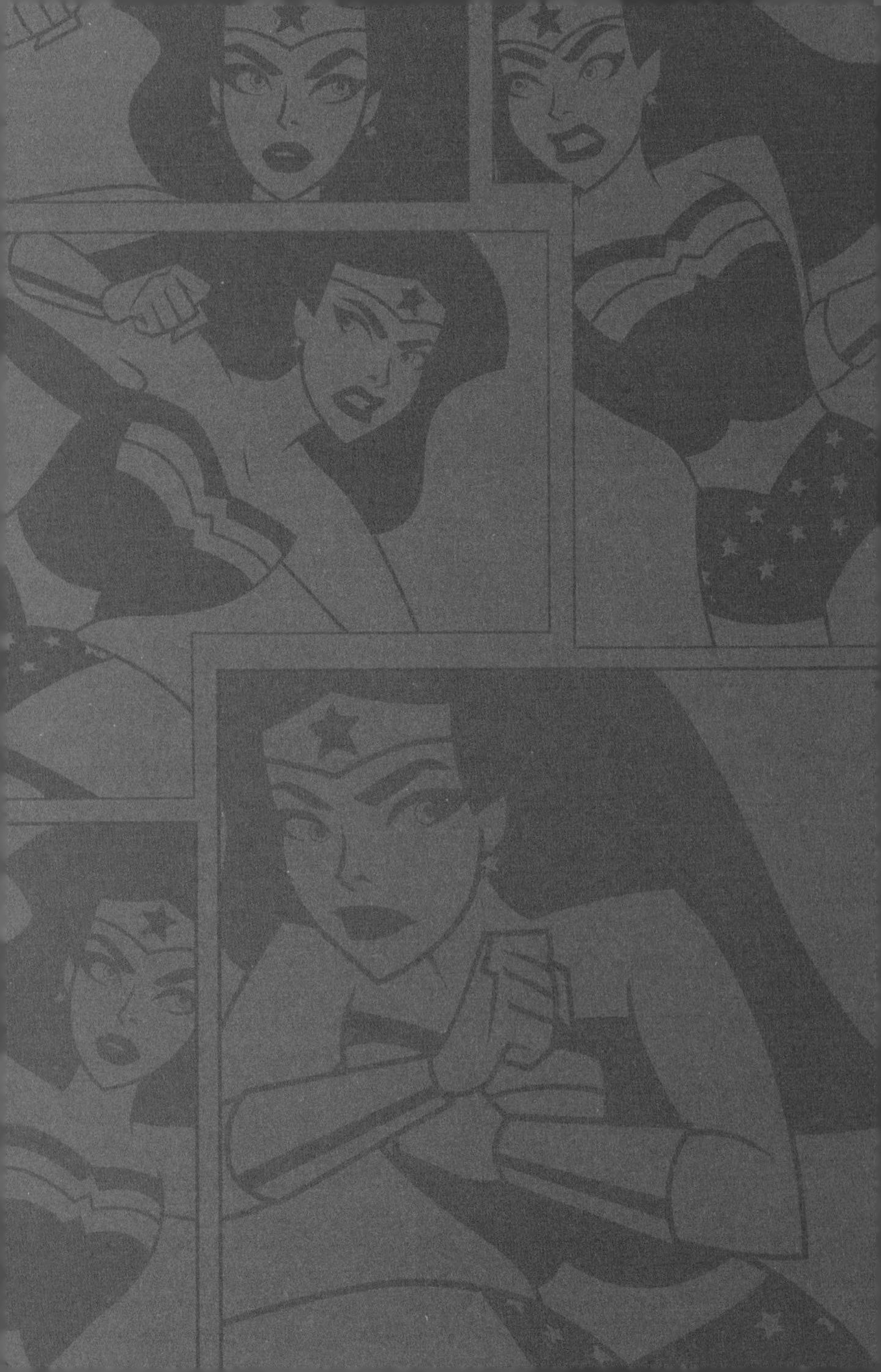

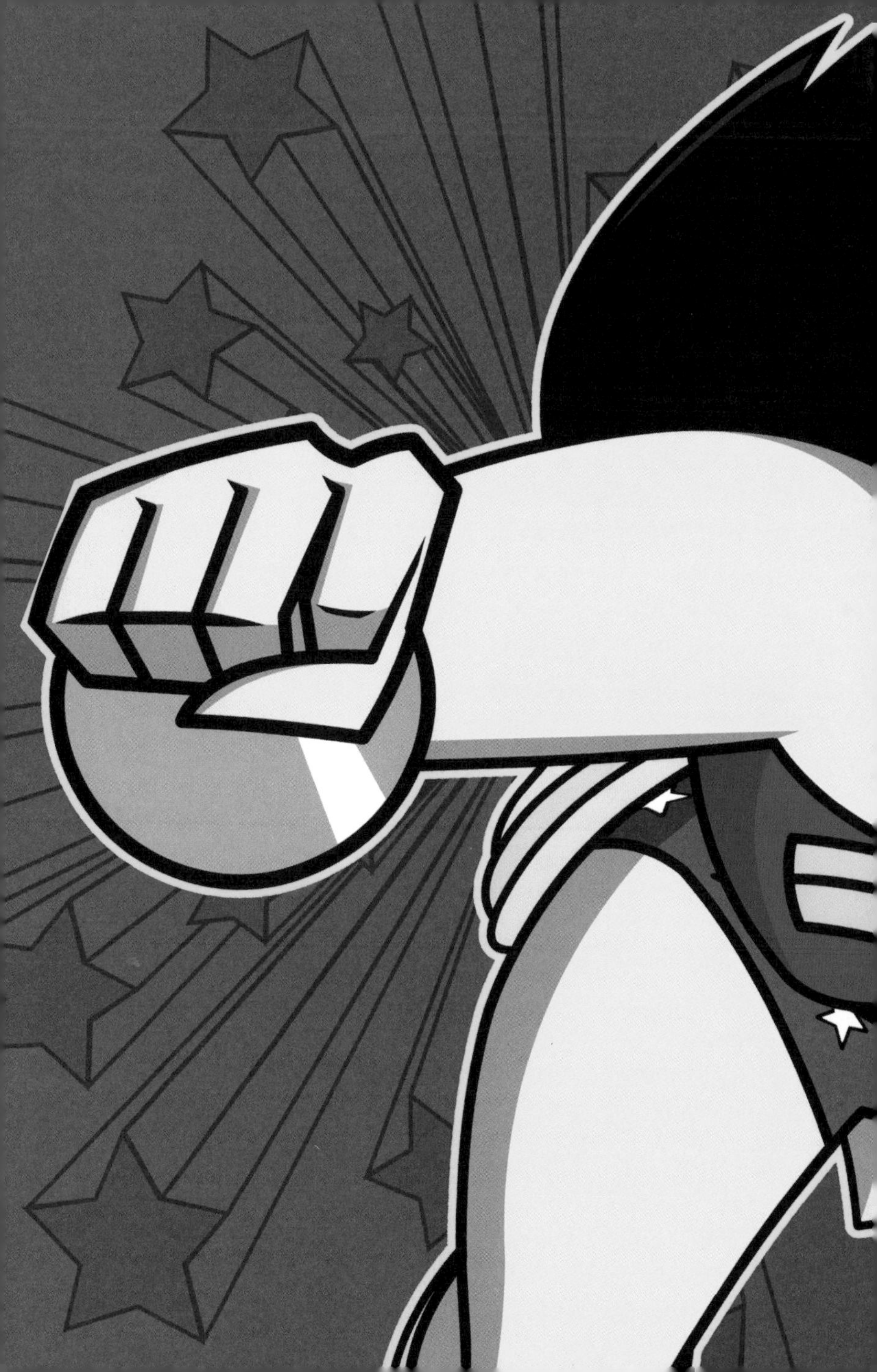

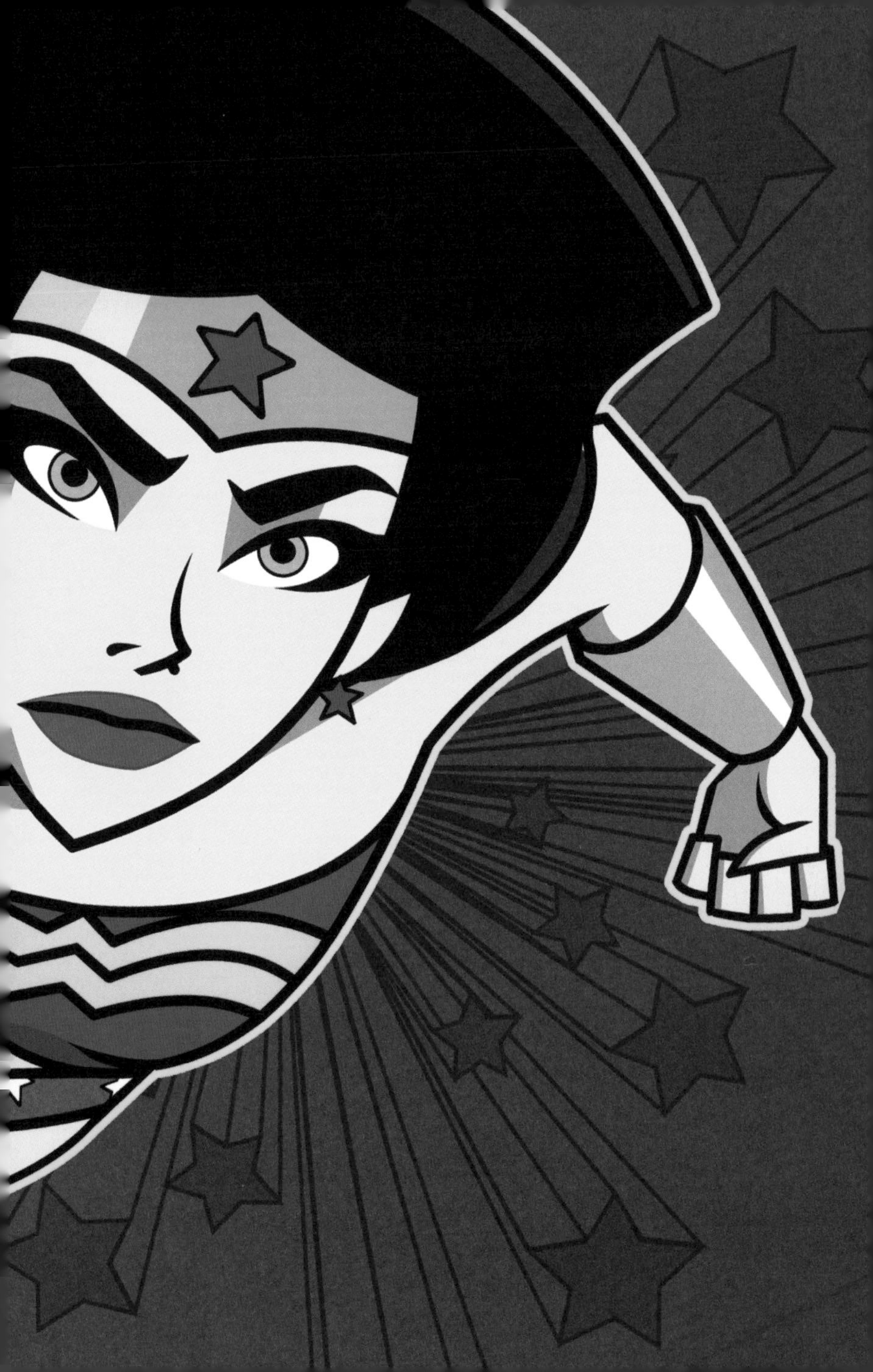

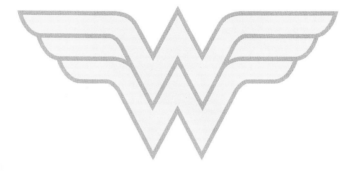